Young MacDonald

by David Milgrim

· DUTTON CHILDREN'S BOOKS ·

DUTTON CHILDREN'S BOOKS

A division of Penguin Young Readers Group • Published by the Penguin Group • Penguin Group (USA) Inc., 375 Hudson Street, New York,
New York 10014, U.S.A. • Penguin Group (Canada), 90 Eglinton Avenue East, Suite 700, Toronto, Ontario, Canada M4P 2Y3 (a division of Pearson Penguin Canada Inc.) • Penguin
Books Ltd, 80 Strand, London WC2R 0RL, England • Penguin Ireland, 25 St Stephen's Green, Dublin 2, Ireland (a division of Penguin Books Ltd) • Penguin Group (Australia),
250 Camberwell Road, Camberwell, Victoria 3124, Australia (a division of Pearson Australia Group Pty Ltd) • Penguin Books India Pvt Ltd, 11 Community Centre, Panchsheel
Park, New Delhi - 110 017, India • Penguin Group (NZ), Cnr Airborne and Rosedale Roads, Albany, Auckland 1310, New Zealand (a division of Pearson New Zealand Ltd) • Penguin
Books (South Africa) (Pty) Ltd, 24 Sturdee Avenue, Rosebank, Johannesburg 2196, South Africa • Penguin Books Ltd, Registered Offices: 80 Strand, London WC2R 0RL, England

CIP Data is available.

Published in the United States by Dutton Children's Books,
a division of Penguin Young Readers Group
345 Hudson Street, New York, New York 10014
www.penguin.com/youngreaders

Designed by Irene Vandervoort

Manufactured in China   First Edition

ISBN 0-525-47570-2

1 3 5 7 9 10 8 6 4 2

For Kendra

Young MacDonald had a farm,
Ee-i-ee-i-o.

And on that farm he made . . . .

A **Hig!** Ee-i-ee-i-o.

With an **Oink-Neigh** here,
And an **Oink-Neigh** there,
Here an **Oink**, there a **Neigh**,
Everywhere an **Oink-Neigh**.
Young MacDonald had a farm,
Ee-i-ee-i-o.

Young MacDonald had a farm, ee-i-ee-i-o.
And on that farm, he made some **Deese,** ee-i-ee-i-o.
With a **Hee-Honk** here,
And a **Hee-Honk** there,
Here a **Hee,** there a **Honk,**
Everywhere a **Hee-Honk.**
Young MacDonald had a farm,
Ee-i-ee-i-o.

Young MacDonald had
A farm, ee-i-ee-i-o.
And on that farm, he
Made a **Shicken,**
Ee-i-ee-i-o.

With a **Baak-Baa** here,
And a **Baak-Baa** there,
Here a **Baak**, there a **Baa**,
Everywhere a **Baak-Baa**.
Young MacDonald had a farm,
Ee-i-ee-i-o.

Young MacDonald had a farm, ee-i-ee-i-o.
And on that farm, he made some **Mucks,** ee-i-ee-i-o.
With a **Quack-Squeak** here,
And a **Quack-Squeak** there,
Here a **Quack,** there a **Squeak,**
Everywhere a **Quack-Squeak.**
Young MacDonald had a farm,
Ee-i-ee-i-o.

Young MacDonald had a farm, ee-i-ee-i-o.
And on that farm, he made a **Cowl,** ee-i-ee-i-o.
With a **Moo-Hoo** here,
And a **Moo-Hoo** there,
Here a **Moo,** there a **Hoo,**
Everywhere a **Moo-Hoo.**
Young MacDonald had a farm,
Ee-i-ee-i-o.

With an **Oops-Arf** here,
And an **Oops-Arf** there,
Here an **Oops**, there an **Arf**,
Everywhere an **Oops-Arf**.
Young MacDonald had a farm,

Ee-i-ee-i-o.

Young MacDonald had a farm, ee-i-ee-i-o.

And on that farm, he made...

Things right!

Ee-i-ee-i-o.

With an **Oink-Oink** here, and a **Neigh-Neigh** there,
Here a **Hee**, there a **Honk**,
Here a **Baak**, there a **Baa**,
Here a **Quack**, there a **Squeak**,
Here a **Moo**, there a **Hoo**,
Everywhere an **Arf-Arf**.

Young MacDonald had a farm, ee-i-ee-i-o.